THE RUNAWAY BUNNY

THE
RUNAWAY BUNNY

by Margaret Wise Brown
Pictures by Clement Hurd

WITH A 75TH ANNIVERSARY RETROSPECTIVE
by Leonard S. Marcus

HARPER
An Imprint of HarperCollinsPublishers

"The Runaway Bunny: A 75th Anniversary Retrospective" by Leonard S. Marcus
Copyright © 2017 by HarperCollins Publishers
Additional retrospective material credits for page 41: illustration from the 1942 edition of *The Runaway Bunny*
(courtesy of Thacher Hurd).

The Runaway Bunny
Copyright © 1942 by Harper & Row, Publishers, Inc.
Text copyright © renewed 1970 by Roberta Brown Rauch
Illustrations copyright © 1972 by Edith T. Hurd, Clement Hurd, John Thacher Hurd, and George
Hellyer, as Trustees of the Edith and Clement Hurd 1982 Trust

ISBN 978-0-06-248994-4

16 17 18 19 20   SCP   10 9 8 7 6 5 4 3 2 1

Revised edition, 2017

THE RUNAWAY BUNNY

Once there was a little bunny who wanted to run away.
So he said to his mother, "I am running away."
"If you run away," said his mother, "I will run after you.
For you are my little bunny."

"If you run after me," said the little bunny,
"I will become a fish in a trout stream
and I will swim away from you."

"If you become a fish in a trout stream," said his mother,
"I will become a fisherman and I will fish for you."

"If you become a fisherman," said the little bunny,
"I will become a rock on the mountain, high above you."

"If you become a rock on the mountain high above me,"
said his mother, "I will be a mountain climber,
and I will climb to where you are."

"If you become a mountain climber,"
said the little bunny,
"I will be a crocus in a hidden garden."

"If you become a crocus in a hidden garden,"
said his mother, "I will be a gardener. And I will find you."

"If you are a gardener and find me,"
said the little bunny, "I will be a bird
and fly away from you."

"If you become a bird and fly away from me,"
said his mother, "I will be a tree that you come home to."

"If you become a tree," said the little bunny,
"I will become a little sailboat,
and I will sail away from you."

"If you become a sailboat and sail away from me,"
said his mother, "I will become the wind
and blow you where I want you to go."

"If you become the wind and blow me," said the little bunny,
"I will join a circus and fly away on a flying trapeze."

"If you go flying on a flying trapeze," said his mother,
"I will be a tightrope walker,
and I will walk across the air to you."

"If you become a tightrope walker and walk across the air,"
said the bunny, "I will become a little boy
and run into a house."

"If you become a little boy and run into a house,"
said the mother bunny, "I will become your mother
and catch you in my arms and hug you."

"Shucks," said the bunny, "I might just as well
stay where I am and be your little bunny."

And so he did.

"Have a carrot," said the mother bunny.

A 75th Anniversary Retrospective

by Leonard S. Marcus

There comes a time in every young child's life when the sheltering embrace of the Great Green Room of *Goodnight Moon* no longer satisfies, and the larger world calls out with the promise of adventure, a promise tinged—at first—with a healthy dose of self-doubt and trepidation. It was for this child that Margaret Wise Brown wrote *The Runaway Bunny*, an intensely felt fable about one of childhood's first big emotional hurdles, and a picture book of surpassing lyricism.

Margaret Wise Brown in Vinalhaven, Maine. *(Photo by Consuelo Kanaga {American, 1894–1978}. Margaret Wise Brown. Cellulose acetate negative, 2½ x 2½ in. (6.4 x 6.4 cm). Brooklyn Museum, Gift of Wallace B. Putnam from the Estate of Consuelo Kanaga, 82.65.1833)*

Brown, at the time, was a charismatic thirty-two-year-old and a rising star in a field into which she had drifted by chance only a few years earlier. A storyteller from childhood, she had come to Greenwich Village after college with vague dreams of literary glory. But when a string of *New Yorker* rejections dashed all hope in that direction, she pivoted to her fallback plan and enrolled in the teacher-training program of New York's progressive Bureau of Educational Experiments—now the Bank Street College of Education.

Founded in 1916 by visionary educational reformer Lucy Sprague Mitchell, the Bureau combined a nursery school, research center, and school for teachers, and prided itself on its independent spirit and experience-based approach to teaching and learning. Rather than lecture Brown and her classmates about children's books, Mitchell challenged them to write stories of their own, then test their work on the nursery school "guinea pigs." When Brown's first assignments revealed a raw but major talent, Mitchell seized the chance to realize one of her lifelong goals. Years of research had convinced her that the standard fare

Lucy Sprague Mitchell's innovative 1921 collection of model stories for young children became a much talked about bestseller. (*Courtesy of the Bank Street College Archives, Bank Street College of Education*)

Lucy Sprague Mitchell, about 1920. (*Courtesy of the Bank Street College Archives, Bank Street College of Education*)

then being published for young children—the
once-upon-a-time picture book tales favored
by librarians at story hour—meant far less
to them than would stories set in the "here
and now" realm of their own experience.
Speaking up in direct opposition to the
New York Public Library's influential authority on
the subject, Anne Carroll Moore, Mitchell argued
not only for stories with modern-day settings but also
for clearly patterned, gamelike narratives that invited
children's direct participation. Recognizing Brown's
potential to become the first "real writer" of the Here
and Now, she mentored and cajoled her mercurial,
sometimes hard-to-manage protégée, helped secure
publication opportunities for her, and in 1938 appointed
Brown as the editor of a small new publishing company
that Mitchell herself had coaxed into existence.

Decorative bench with rabbit motif designed by Clement Hurd for the family of Michael and Jane Hare and embroidered by Jane Hare, late 1930s. *(Courtesy of Susan Howe on behalf of Jane Jopling Hare)*

It was in her role as William R. Scott, Inc.'s editor that
Brown first met Clement Hurd, a painter and decorative artist whose playful, Fauve-inflected
murals for a friend's Connecticut country house had suggested to her an illustrator in the making.
Soon Hurd and Brown (the latter in one or both of her dual roles as Scott's editor and prolific

The Orleans, Massachusetts, wedding of Clement Hurd and Edith Thacher, on June 24, 1939—days before Gertrude Stein's *The World Is Round* went to press. (*Courtesy of Thacher Hurd*)

author) happily embarked on a handful of thrillingly original book projects, all inspired by Mitchell's revolutionary ideas. In 1939, the artist married another Scott author, Edith Thacher, and illustrated a book that briefly propelled the tiny new firm into the national spotlight: Gertrude Stein's first work for children, *The World Is Round*.

Under Mitchell's tutelage, Brown blossomed into a

Illustration by Clement Hurd for the 1939 edition of *The World Is Round*. Hurd redrew the art for the 1967 edition also published by Scott. (*Copyright © 1939, renewed 1966 by Clement Hurd*)

disciplined and astonishingly productive writer who, while also maintaining a whirlwind social life, seemed to Hurd and other colleagues always to be writing. The first glimmerings of *The Runaway Bunny* came to her over the summer of 1940 while she vacationed on Vinalhaven, a densely forested island in Maine's luminous Penobscot Bay. From her perch in a tumbledown rented seaside cottage, Brown, in a letter to Mitchell, reflected on the expanding war in Europe and Asia, then let Mitchell in on her latest writing experiment: "Don't you hate to see this summer go? With the world in such a fireworks of horror it seems like the last summer. I seem to cling to it as such." She had come across a medieval French love poem, the strong, simple "if . . . then" pattern of which, Brown continued, seemed ready-made "for our ends . . . I may use it in a picture book," Brown teased her, "so beat me to it."

The ballad that had so intrigued Brown characterized a lover's pursuit of his beloved as a hunt involving a series of magical transformations:

> If you pursue me I shall become a fish in the water
>
> And I shall escape you
>
> If you become a fish I shall become an eel
>
> And I shall eat you
>
> If you become an eel I shall become a fox . . .

Variations on the theme abound in the Western poetic tradition. Consider, for example, Old Testament Psalm 139 ("If I take the wings of the morning, and dwell in the uttermost parts of the sea, even there shall thy hand lead me"); or the Greek myth of Peleus and Thetis; or the anonymous seventeenth-century English ballad that reads in part:

> Should his Love become a swallow,
>
> Through the air to stray,
>
> Love will lend wings to follow,
>
> And will find out the way.

For Brown, the vividly imagistic narrative was equally well suited to a dramatization of the developmental battle of wits that every mother and child plays out as the latter first asserts his or her independence.

It amused Brown's friends that she not only wrote stories about imaginary rabbits but also, as a member of Long Island's Buckram Beagles, hunted real rabbits on weekends. In a *New Yorker* piece for March 8, 1941, titled "Tallyho!," E. J. Kahn Jr. described an "agile friend . . . known in beagling circles as Brownie," who relished the sport and kept a prized rabbit's foot on her writing desk. Brown herself saw no contradiction in any of this. Rather, she took pride (as Beatrix Potter had done before her) in maintaining a rigorously unsentimental view of the children (or, as she preferred to say, "people") she wrote for, whom she regarded as rabbity in their quick-witted responsiveness to life in the face of their extreme vulnerability. Cuteness had nothing to do with why, in the end, Brown identified so fervently with the doughty heroes of her poignant, sly, and deceptively simple tales.

Ursula Nordstrom, who directed Harper's children's book department from 1940 to 1973. *(Erich Hartmann, Magnum Photos)*

Over the next months, she completed two drafts of *The Runaway Bunny*, sold the manuscript to Harper & Brothers (a much larger firm than Scott, and one with which she had already published a handful of books), and persuaded her editor there, Ursula Nordstrom, to hire Clement Hurd to illustrate it.[1] The usually voluble Nordstrom was always a bit awestruck around the glamorous author she dubbed "Miss Genius." Writing to

---

1. Brown's career developed so rapidly that by 1941 she had at least five publishers vying for her picture books.

Brown in Maine that summer, she summoned her courage to request a stronger ending. Brown's swift reply came by telegram: "'Have a carrot,' said the mother bunny." A parting wink to the reader, the new closing line was the perfect release from the emotional intensity of the contest of wits that had come before it.

Brown, however, was not ready to let the manuscript go. Writing to Mitchell that October from Vermont, where Clement Hurd and his wife were now living, she once again sought her mentor's "poetic criticism": "I wallow in uncertainty about punctuation, wording, and form. Whether I should use *If you will become*, or, *If you are I will be* or mix them both up so that the rhythm gets broken from page to page and isn't so soporific, or what is consistency and what makes the best poetry and if what makes the best poetry isn't more for even a small child than concessions to clarity."

In Nordstrom's office a month later, Brown scribbled comments for forwarding to Hurd as she reviewed his latest work: "Feel the jacket cover isn't up to the inside of the book . . . It looks scraggly and not quite finished or maybe it is that the bunny personalities don't come through the

Brown scribbled these notes, for forwarding to Clement Hurd, in Ursula Nordstrom's office on November 19, 1941. *(Courtesy of Thacher Hurd and Hollins University. Used by permission of WaterMark, Inc.)*

grass . . . Mother bunny's rump got elongated like a blimp again. Haunches don't come to a point. I like the relationship between the two bunnies."

Hurd's plan called for two complementary sets of illustrations: wordless full-color paintings for the bunnies' extravagant transformation scenes, alternating with simpler line drawings of the rabbit mother and child for the pages with text. It was standard practice in those days of prohibitive color-printing costs to limit an illustrator's options, if color was to be allowed at all. Hurd turned the situation to brilliant advantage by using his color allotment to dramatize the contrast between reality and make-believe.

Turning to the newly arrived line drawings, which on the whole she liked, Brown continued to poke and prod: "Why can't a crocus have crocus leaves and why does the mother find a daisy on the next page (daisies grow in the summer).

Watch your bunny anatomy. I keep seeing traces of a Kerry Blue puppy"—her favorite breed of dog—"and of a line in a hurry." Careful to end on a high note, she urged her friend not to "forget this is our chef d'oeuvre."

Hurd faced hurdles more daunting than Brown's pinpoint criticisms. As an artist with only a handful of books to his credit, he was a comparative novice at the task of preparing pre-separated art, an exacting process that called upon the illustrator to analyze and chart each color illustration in terms of the four individual printer's inks to be used for reproduction. For every illustration, a "separation," or schematic drawing, was needed for each of the four inks (cyan, magenta, yellow, and black). From these, the printer's plates were made, and any miscalculation might throw off the outcome.

By late November, Hurd had completed the work for all but the cover design and received the printer's qualified approval. If not "facsimile in value" to the original paintings, the artist

Gouache study for the 1942 edition inspired by Georges Seurat's *The Circus*, featuring a bareback rider. *(Courtesy of the Margaret Wise Brown Papers, Kerlan Collection, Children's Literature Research Collections, University of Minnesota Libraries, Minneapolis)*

Gouache illustration for the 1942 edition. *(Courtesy of the Margaret Wise Brown Papers, Kerlan Collection, Children's Literature Research Collections, University of Minnesota Libraries, Minneapolis)*

May Lamberton Becker's upbeat assessment in the March 15, 1942, issue of the *New York Herald-Tribune* was typical of the first reviews. *The Runaway Bunny*'s promise of a mother's unconditional love for her child assumed new meaning for readers in wartime.

was assured, the printed book would at a minimum be "very colorful and attractive."

The first printing of *The Runaway Bunny* was colorful all right, but the garish result was so far from the artist's intention that both he and Brown urged Harper to consider going back to press for a second try. By publication time in March 1942, however, America was at war, and thoughts of repairing the damage had to be set aside indefinitely.

Reviewers, in any case, seemed not to notice the shortcomings of the book's color reproduction. The *New York Herald-Tribune*'s influential critic May Lamberton Becker expressed the majority view: "Pictures and text are in complete collaboration. Brilliant in color, the large scenes show the dreams, while realistic black-and-whites show that this is really a mother-play."

Now events moved swiftly, especially for Hurd. First came a plum April cover assignment from *Town & Country*, for which he designed a poster-like appeal for the purchase of war bonds. The following month, orders arrived for him to report for duty to Jefferson Barracks, Missouri. Hurd was to be commissioned as an army second lieutenant and, like many other artists, assigned to a camouflage unit. He would be dispatched to the Pacific front at Thanksgiving time.

Hurd enlisted in the US Army soon after the attack on Pearl Harbor. This telegram, dated May 14, 1942, gave the artist two weeks to put his affairs in order before reporting for duty. *(Courtesy of Thacher Hurd)*

That fall, it came as no great surprise when the New York Public Library, where Brown's ties to librarian Anne Carroll Moore's nemesis Lucy Sprague Mitchell had almost always counted against her, omitted *The Runaway Bunny* from its bellwether holiday best books list. *The Horn Book*, most likely for similar reasons, had not bothered to review it. Even so, the initial sale of *The Runaway Bunny* was so brisk that Brown, writing to Hurd without knowing for sure whether he was still in the country, predicted that their latest book would "cushion our old age." It was a bittersweet sentiment considering, as she wistfully reminded her friend, that they both were "still in 'our pre-famous period,'" and with no chance now to celebrate their first major shared success, let alone build on it. Three years later, with the war winding down, Brown would write Edith Hurd that she had not lost hope that a new edition of *The Runaway Bunny* might soon be

In the months before he left for the war, Hurd saw the publication not only of *The Runaway Bunny* but also of his first collaboration with his wife "Posey": *Speedy: The Hook & Ladder Truck* (Lothrop, Lee & Shepard, 1942). *(Courtesy of Thacher Hurd)*

Writing to Edith Thacher Hurd in early 1945, Brown restated her wish for a new printing of *The Runaway Bunny* with improved color reproduction and revealed her quirky plan to dedicate a new story collection to that book, which she had long considered a favorite. *(Courtesy of Thacher Hurd and Hollins University. Used by permission of WaterMark, Inc.)*

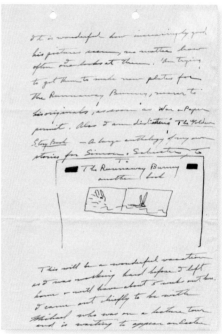

in the offing, adding with a cryptic flourish of the kind that so often left her bemused friends chuckling: "Also I am dedicating *The Golden Story Book*—a large anthology of my own stories for Simon & Schuster—'To *The Runaway Bunny*, another book.'"[2] At Christmastime, when Clement Hurd finally reached New York on his way back home to Vermont, Brown had a fine gift waiting for him: not the wished-for new edition of their last collaboration, but the manuscript for their next one, *Goodnight Moon*.[3]

2. The book referred to was published as *Margaret Wise Brown's Wonderful Story Book: 42 Stories and Poems*, by Margaret Wise Brown, illustrated by J. P. Miller (New York: Simon & Schuster, 1948). The longed-for new *Runaway Bunny* did not come to fruition until 1972. But Nordstrom did expand the original edition, most likely at this same time or soon afterward, by appending the music and lyrics of "The Song of the Runaway Bunny," with Brown's words set to a traditional French melody as arranged by the nineteenth-century musicologist and composer Julien Tiersot.
3. In the finished art for *Goodnight Moon*, Hurd inserted a scene from *The Runaway Bunny* as a framed picture hanging on the wall of the Great Green Room—an early instance of product placement and a sure sign that Brown, Nordstrom, and Hurd saw the two books as closely linked in spirit.

Only forty-two years old when she died in 1952 of an embolism while traveling in France, Margaret Wise Brown just missed seeing *Goodnight Moon*, which Harper published in 1947, become a modern-day publishing phenomenon. Sales of the book took off a year after her death, when the coauthors of a nationally syndicated advice column for mothers, Drs. Frances Ilg and Louise Bates Ames, recommended it to their legions of devoted readers. For the remainder of the baby boom years and beyond, as sales of *Goodnight Moon* spiraled upward and *Runaway Bunny* sales tagged along at a respectable rate, the case for a new edition of the latter book grew steadily stronger. In the fall of 1965, Harper's Ursula Nordstrom was finally game, and invited Hurd to tell her how he might "do [the book] differently." Four months later, Nordstrom had most of Hurd's new color artwork in hand and wrote to express her astonishment at "how BEAUTIFULLY" he had "done [the illustrations] again twenty-five years later" without having lost "one single bit" of

The final "Have a carrot" illustration for the 1942 edition . . .
(Courtesy of the Margaret Wise Brown Papers, Kerlan Collection, Children's Literature Research Collections, University of Minnesota Libraries, Minneapolis)

the spirit of the original book. "In fact you have added to it."

In earlier times, when Hurd was a newcomer to the field with an admittedly wobbly command of his craft, he and Nordstrom had periodically sparred over deadlines, overdue advances, and the like. Now, however, Nordstrom had nothing but praise for the illustrator who in the meantime had also become a dear friend: "I just can't tell you how thrilled I am over all of this," she wrote Hurd. Commenting one by one on the various illustrations, she reached a crescendo of enthusiasm over the final picture: "The new HAVE A CARROT is absolutely stupendously marvelous." Revisiting *The Runaway Bunny* had left the editor in an elegiac mood. "I always loved [this] book so much," she wrote, "and it stood for an awful lot for me—when we were all young and sort of nuts . . . And it is somehow very very reassuring that you've kept all the best of you 25 years ago and combined it with the best of your abilities now." She was certain that Brown would have felt exactly as she did.

. . . and the 1972 illustration, which Hurd had originally painted for Brown's *Wait Till the Moon Is Full* years earlier.

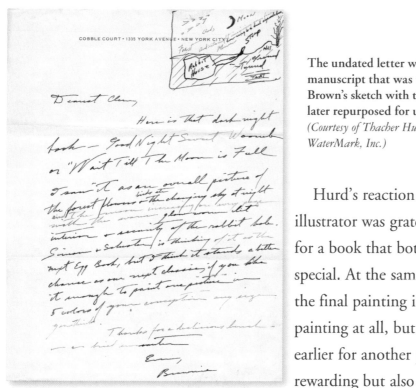

The undated letter with which Brown introduced Hurd to the manuscript that was to have become their "next classic." Compare Brown's sketch with the ill-fated painting (shown on page 55) that Hurd later repurposed for use in the 1972 edition of *The Runaway Bunny*. *(Courtesy of Thacher Hurd and Hollins University. Used by permission of WaterMark, Inc.)*

Hurd's reaction was a bit more complex. The illustrator was grateful for the chance to reimagine the art for a book that both he and Brown had always considered special. At the same time, he savored the knowledge that the final painting in the new batch was not really a new painting at all, but rather one that he had done years earlier for another picture book from which Brown—a rewarding but also difficult professional partner—had summarily dismissed him mid-collaboration.

Envisioned by Brown as a companion to *The Runaway Bunny*, *Wait Till the Moon Is Full* told the story of a slightly older child who, having shed his ambivalence about letting go of his mother's protection, was keenly determined to strike

Illustration by Garth Williams for *Wait Till the Moon Is Full*, written by Margaret Wise Brown, a book that Brown had first considered Hurd for as the illustrator. *(Copyright © 1948 by Margaret Wise Brown, renewed 1976 by Garth Williams)*

Ink drawing by Clement Hurd for the 1942 edition.

out on his own. Brown wrote the story at a time when she herself had ventured into new emotional territory and become deeply involved in a love affair with a woman she revered but whom Hurd was convinced was treating her badly. Brown idolized Blanche Oelrichs, a charismatic poet and lecturer known to the world by the penname Michael Strange. But Hurd was distressed by the cruelty with which Strange belittled Brown for (among other things) writing poetry for children, and he spoke up about it. When Brown noticed that another of her favorite illustrators, Garth Williams, got along perfectly well with Michael Strange, she turned *Wait Till the Moon Is Full* over to him. To make the book his own, Williams gamely recast the rabbit characters as badgers. Hurd's new "Have a carrot" illustration that

Sketch by Hurd for the parallel illustration for the 1972 edition. *(Courtesy of the Margaret Wise Brown Papers, Kerlan Collection, Children's Literature Research Collections, University of Minnesota Libraries, Minneapolis)*

Nordstrom so admired had originally been painted for this other book, which Harper published with Williams's notably restrained illustrations in 1948.

Final ink drawing for the 1972 edition.

The new paintings on Nordstrom's desk were the work of an illustrator who had grown enormously in twenty-five years. The earlier versions had a characteristically warm and playful spirit, and flashes of inspiration: the mother rabbit as jaunty alpine adventurer, wind goddess, and best of all, topiary rabbit-tree. But Hurd had often been unsure just how and where to position his characters, and their faces had often lacked conviction. The new color illustrations had a much tighter emotional focus and a stronger sense of design. The smaller black-and-white drawings—still to be redone for the new edition—were blocky and awkward. The next step was for Hurd to redo them too, which he proceeded to do on into the spring.

Hurd's wait was far from over, however. A flurry of original projects slowed his progress, and the steady sale of the old edition made some at Harper question the need for a new one. By 1970, rising production costs and an industry-wide downturn added to the list of negatives. When the redesigned and reillustrated *The Runaway Bunny* finally took its bow in the spring of 1972, Harper was able to tout it as the thirtieth anniversary edition of a beloved classic. Happily, reviewers treated it as a new book rather than as a mere reissue as Nordstrom—ever the worrier—had feared. That November, the *New York Times Book Review* listed it as one of the year's notable children's books. It has continued to grow in renown ever since.

Most striking about *The Runaway Bunny*'s legacy is its recurring role as a pop-cultural touchstone. In 1979, as the national divorce rate approached its historic high, *Kramer vs. Kramer*, the story of a bitter custody battle, won the Academy Award for the year's best picture. In it (as in the bestselling novel by Avery Corman on which the film was based), the child who is caught in the middle of

The Runaway Bunny is featured in *Kramer vs. Kramer*, which won the 1979 Academy Award for Best Picture.

the dispute pointedly asks his father to read him *The Runaway Bunny*, with its promise of a mother who will never abandon her son. In the logic of the film's story, a children's book that in happier times had ranked as one among many bedtime favorites had come to represent a lifeline.

During the 1980s and 1990s, the divorce rate remained high but America also experienced a second postwar baby boom, with a new wave of parents who belonged to history's best-educated, most book-minded generation. Atlanta kindergarten teacher turned playwright Margaret Edson could count on many in her audience to know a "classic" picture book like *The Runaway Bunny* when she inserted it as a key plot point in *Wit*, the 1999 Pulitzer Prize winner in Drama. (It too became an award-winning film.) Near the end of Edson's play, Dr. Vivian Bearing, a literature professor who is dying of cancer, is visited by her mentor, Dr. E. M. Ashford. The older woman happens to have with her a copy of *The Runaway Bunny* as a gift for her great-grandson. An authority on the English metaphysical poets, Bearing has lived for intellectual rigor all

The Runaway Bunny also plays a part in Margaret Edson's 1999 Pulitzer Prize–winning drama *Wit*. An Emmy Award–winning cable television adaptation followed in 2001.

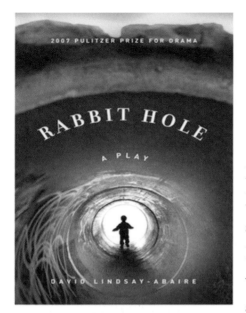

2007 PULITZER PRIZE FOR DRAMA

RABBIT HOLE

A PLAY

DAVID LINDSAY-ABAIRE

In 2008, David Lindsay Abaire's *Rabbit Hole* became the second play in which *The Runaway Bunny* serves as a pop cultural touchstone to win the Pulitzer Prize in Drama.

her professional life. But now, in her final hours, she opts to hear her former teacher read to her not from the Donne sonnets she so assiduously parsed and pondered over the years, but rather from Brown's forthright, bell-clear lyric: "Once there was a little bunny who wanted to run away. . . ." Pausing mid-reading, Ashford is suddenly transfixed by the unforeseen depths of Margaret Wise Brown's blithe literary creation. "Look at that," she gasps in amazement, "a little allegory of the soul. Wherever it [the bunny child] hides, God will find it. . . . Wonderful."

Curiously, the 2007 Pulitzer Prize winner in Drama, David Lindsay-Abaire's *Rabbit Hole*, also takes *The Runaway Bunny* as a cultural signpost. In the course of anatomizing the grief of a once self-satisfied suburban couple following the death of their young son, the play lays bare the landscape of a contemporary parenting style marked by wildly exaggerated parental fears and expectations. None of the couple's earnest efforts could prevent the freak automobile accident that killed their son. In the aftermath of their loss, *The Runaway Bunny*—one of the bedtime books with which they too had dutifully stocked their child's bookshelf—comes back to haunt them as a seeming rebuke for having failed to measure up as their child's ultimate protectors.

Millennial parents would come to be known, and satirized, for the earnest determination with

This *New Yorker* magazine Sketchbook by Roz Chast ran in the double issue for February 23 and March 2, 2015. *(Roz Chast/The* New Yorker *Collection/The Cartoon Bank)*

which they micromanaged their young children's overscheduled lives. Viewed this way, Brown's mother rabbit could seem the ultimate "helicopter parent," as Roz Chast gleefully deadpanned in a *New Yorker* Sketchbook. For cartoonist Harry Bliss, *The Runaway Bunny* offered the perfect opportunity for exposing the dark side of parental involvement taken to such extremes. In Bliss's caption for a parody of Clement Hurd's familiar cover image, a burned-out mother rabbit coldly orders her dumbstruck bunny to "Get lost." So much for unconditional love!

Adults are forever remapping the emotional terrain comprised of childhood's opposing needs for security and freedom. In illuminating that territory, Brown and Hurd gave us a tale that is every bit as resilient as its dueling protagonists. Parenting styles come and go, as do so many picture books. But for seventy-five years now, readers have found in *The Runaway Bunny* a story they need.

FOREIGN LANGUAGE FIRST EDITIONS OF *THE RUNAWAY BUNNY*

1978	Japanese (Holp Shuppan Ltd.)
1997	Complex Chinese (HsinYi Publications)
1998	Hebrew (Sifriat Maariv)
1999	French (Mijade Edition)
2001	Hmong (Minnesota Humanities Commission)
2005	Simplified Chinese (Hsinex International Corp.)
2005	Spanish (HarperCollins)
2009	Korean (Prooni Books, Inc.)
2011	Russian (Pink Giraffe Publishing)
2016	Thai (Siam Cement Foundation)
Forthcoming	Vietnamese (Quangvan Books)
Forthcoming	German (Diogenes Verlag)
Forthcoming	Romanian (Editura Art)